Hornetto

Violet

Slugsy

Aunt Tulip

Grubby

Mo

Bumble

Created by Keith Chapman

First published in Great Britain by HarperCollins Children's Books in 2008

1 3 5 7 9 10 8 6 4 2

ISBN-13: 978-0-00-727507-6

A CIP catalogue record for this title is available from the British Library.

Based on the television series Fifi and the Flowertots, © Chapman Entertainment Limited 2008

Visit Fifi at www.Fifiandtheflowertots.com

Printed and bound in Italy
by Rotolito Lombarda Spa

Fifi and the Flowertots
Annual 2009

HarperCollins *Children's Books*

Contents

Hello there, I'm Fifi Forget-Me-Not!

Would you like to hear a story about
the time my lovely friends threw
me a party? Or the day I baked
some yummy bread, but lost
some ingredients?

As well as the stories, there are lots
of games and fun things to do in this
Flowertot Annual. And there are some
lovely pictures to fill with your
favourite colours, too!

I think one of my favourite things
to do is making rainbow bubbles,
but you might like some of
the other activities better.

First, though, why don't you read along
with me about my special
happy day party?

Fifi's Happy Day

One sunny day, Fifi was weeding her garden when Primrose and Violet arrived with some news.

"Fifi! You're going to have a party,"

they laughed.

"But why?" asked Fifi in surprise, "It's not my birthday!"

"You don't need
to have a birthday
to have a party!"
said Primrose.
"Leave it all to me.
Come to Poppy's
market stall at
teatime – and wear
your best dress!"
And with that,
off they went.

Primrose planned the party very carefully. She made a list of all the things that needed to be done, and put the name of the Flowertot whose job it was next to each one.

"Stingo and Slugsy, I'd like you to make the cake for Fifi's party. Don't make a mess," Primrose told them. And off she went.

9

Fifi's friends were all having fun,
busily preparing for her party, but Fifi didn't
want to spoil the surprise for herself!
But what could she do while she was
waiting for the party to start?

Suddenly, Fifi had an idea. "I know," she said, "I'll bake a cake to take to the party!"

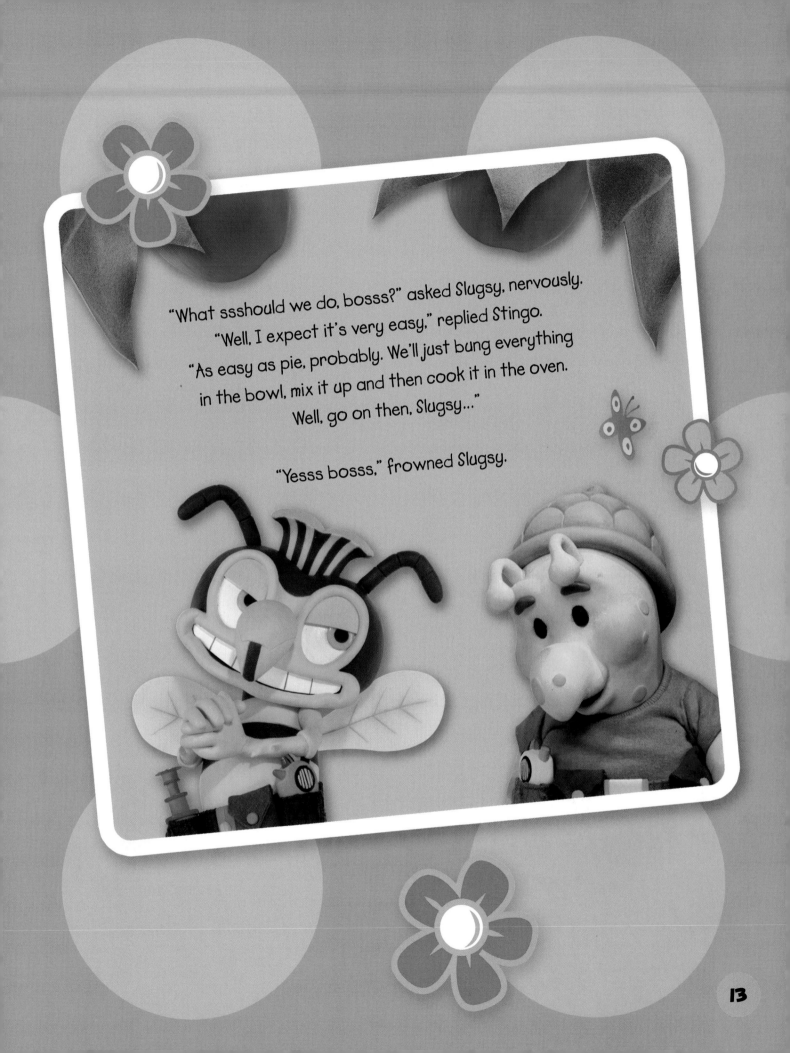

"What ssshould we do, bosss?" asked Slugsy, nervously.
"Well, I expect it's very easy," replied Stingo.
"As easy as pie, probably. We'll just bung everything
in the bowl, mix it up and then cook it in the oven.
Well, go on then, Slugsy..."

"Yesss bosss," frowned Slugsy.

Fifi's baking was going very well. Her chocolate cake was now in the oven and she had just finished cleaning her kitchen.

Primrose's kitchen, on the other hand, was anything but clean!
Stingo and Slugsy had managed to get cake mixture
all over the place.

"Hopping hollyhocks! You two can jolly well clear this lot up right now!" she said, frostily. "Your cake had better be worth all this mess!"

Fifi's cake turned out beautifully, as usual.
And Stingo and Slugsy looked pretty pleased
with their efforts.
"Obviously, a wasp
of my talent
can turn his hand
to most things..."
said Stingo.

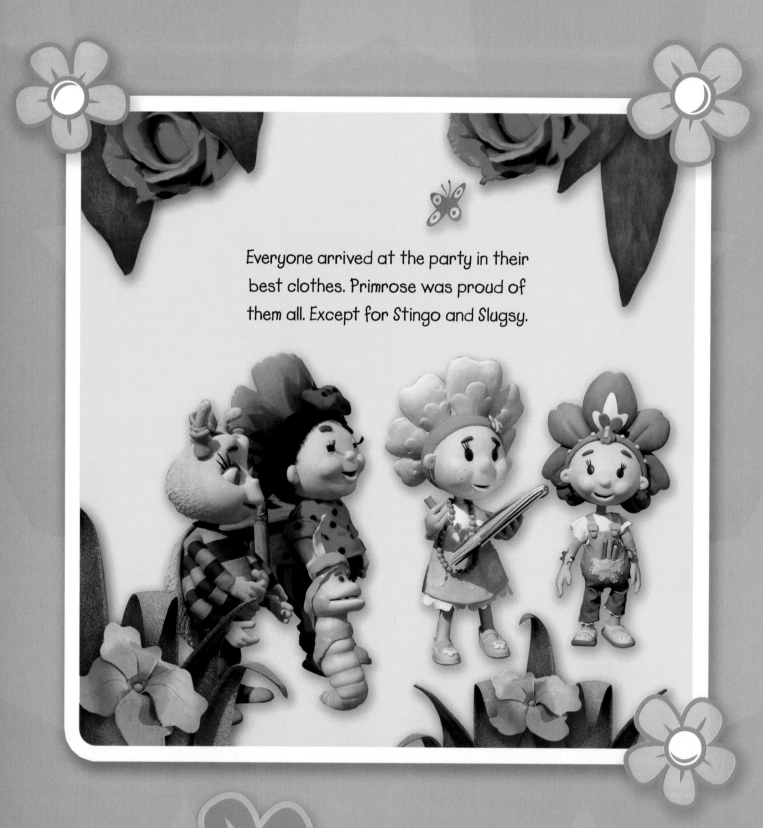

Everyone arrived at the party in their best clothes. Primrose was proud of them all. Except for Stingo and Slugsy.

"What kind of a cake do you call that?" Primrose snapped at them. "It's burnt, it's flat and it's got eggshells in it!"

"Sssorry, Primrose," said Slugsy. "We did our bessst." Just then, Fifi arrived at the party.

"Hello, everyone," she said, "I've made you all a cake to say thank you for giving me this Happy Day party! I hope you like it."

Primrose's frown disappeared. "Thank you, Fifi," she said delightedly. "Now that's what I call a proper cake."

By the end of the party
all the Tots were tired out.

"Thank you
all so much for the
party," smiled Fifi,
"it's really made
my Happy Day!"

Rainbow Tag

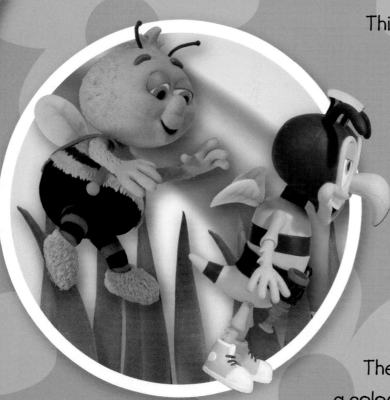

This is a great game and all the running around keeps you warm outdoors on a cold day!

Choose one person to be 'It'. This person will chase the others and when he or she touches another player, that player is out.

The person who is 'It' chooses a colour to be 'safe'. If any player is touching an object of that colour, they are safe and cannot be caught. But if another person comes and touches the same object, they become safe instead, and the other person must move.

It's more fun if you choose a different colour for each round.

Players' clothes do not count!

All players try to avoid being caught, and the last player left becomes 'It' for the next round.

All Change

We love playing All Change in Flowertot Garden!

Everyone stands in a circle, and someone is chosen to be the leader. The leader starts an action – clapping, for example, and everyone joins in as soon as they see what he or she is doing.

When the leader changes the action, everybody must follow as quickly as they can. The last person to change to the new action is out.

The game continues until only one person besides the leader is still playing, and that person becomes the new leader. Everybody joins in again and follows the actions of the new leader.

Actions can include all sorts of things, such as jumping up and down, hopping on one leg, patting your head, bunny hops or even singing a nursery rhyme (but make sure it's one you all know!)

Bumble's Bubbles

Blowing bubbles is great fun, and Bumble has
a really easy recipe for bubble mix.

You will need:

1 tablespoon glycerine
2 tablespoons washing-up liquid
9 fluid oz (0.25 litre) water

Mix all the ingredients together gently.
Pour the bubble mix into a bowl or tray
that you can easily dip your bubble wand into.

Make a bubble wand

You can make a bubble wand out of almost anything.
All you need is a handle and a loop to dip in the bubble mix.

Try cutting the centre out of
a round yogurt or margarine tub lid,
and taping it to a pencil for a handle.

Different sized wands make different sized
bubbles. You might need to try blowing
harder or more gently with different
wands to get the best bubbles.

A Rainbow Bubble

Make a beautiful rainbow-coloured
bubble either indoors or outdoors.

You will need:
A torch with a flat bottom,
so that you can stand it upright
with the light pointing upwards
Bubble mix
A clear plastic lid
A drinking straw

✿ Put the lid on top of the torch, so that
the rim of the lid is upwards.

✿ Put some bubble mix on the lid. 1 tablespoon should be enough.

✿ Use the straw to spread the bubble solution all over the lid.

✿ Use the dry end of the straw to blow a bubble into the lid.

✿ The light from the torch makes a beautiful, colourful bubble.

✿ If you can't see it well enough, try turning the lights down
or, if you're outside, wait until the sun goes down.

Imaginary Hide and Seek

You can play this game anywhere, and it's especially good for when you're on a long journey somewhere! Mo and I sometimes play it when we're driving around Flowertot garden!

✿ Find one to three friends.

✿ Pick somewhere with lots of hiding places that everyone knows. It could be your garden, a room in your house or at school, or a playground, for example.

✿ Each person thinks of the place where they would hide.

✿ Then everyone takes turns guessing where the person on their left is hiding.

✿ Everyone must be honest and say when he or she is 'found', but everyone can keep asking questions until the last person is found!

Variation: You could pretend that you are different sizes for some games – for example the size of a mouse, or a cat. Being a different size means you can hide in all sorts of different hiding places!

Colour Collect

Violet loves this game. She chooses the brightest colours of wool she can to be sure they're not too hard to find!

❀ Find some wool of four or five different colours.

❀ Cut into short lengths, about 10 inches (25 cm) long. Make sure that there are enough pieces of each colour for all the players, but keep them in bundles of the same colour for now.

❀ Ask an adult, or someone who is not playing the game, to hide each bundle of coloured wool separately in the playing area.

❀ Everyone tries to find one length of all the colours of wool. The first person to have a full set wins!

❀ If you have a lot of people, say at a birthday party, it's even more fun if one person takes each bundle of coloured wool and hides with it. Then they can tie the wool on to the finders' wrists as bracelets.

Who am I?

This is a lovely game where people have to ask and answer questions about me and my Flowertot friends!

How to play:

✿ Copy and colour as many of these Flowertots as you need (one for each player) on blank pieces of paper, and cut them out carefully.

✿ Keeping the pictures hidden, tape one on to each person's back. Ask someone else to tape one to you first, so that you don't know which one it is either.

✿ You can take turns asking each other questions (only ones that can be answered with 'yes' or 'no'), or you can move around, asking different people questions about the person or character you are, until you guess the correct answer!

Baking Day

One day Fifi got up and looked out of the window of Forget-Me-Not Cottage. It was raining hard outside. "Fiddly Flowerpetals," she said to herself, "This will be lovely for the plants, but it's not so good for me. I think I'll stay indoors and bake a lovely loaf of bread for tea."

She went downstairs to find Bumble
was already in the kitchen,
shaking himself dry.
"It's too wet for me today, Fifi," he said.
"Do you mind if I stay here with you?"
"Of course you can stay here, Bumble,"
replied Fifi.
"I'm going to make some fresh bread
for tea. We can have it with some
of your delicious honey!"
"Good idea, Fifi!" said Bumble.
"What do you need to make bread?"
"Well, we'll need some flour,"
said Fifi, looking in the cupboard and
taking out a big bag. "And some
salt, water and yeast, to make
it nice and light. I know! We could
put in lots of lovely seeds and
grains, to make it really tasty!"
"Sounds good to me," said Bumble, smiling.
"Can I do anything to help?"
"Yes, please, Bumble," said Fifi.
"I'll mix up the other ingredients,
and you could look in the cupboards
and get out all the yummy seeds
you can find to go in the bread."

Fifi began mixing everything together to make the bread. Bumble
looked in all Fifi's cupboards and found lots of different kinds of seeds.
"Here you are, Fifi," he said, putting the jars on the table in front of her.
"Buttercups and daisies, Bumble, you've found lots!
Poppy seeds are very tasty – we'll put some of those in. And sesame seeds.
Ooh, and my favourite! Sunflower seeds! They'll make it look nice."
Fifi tipped the bread dough on to the table and put a handful
of each of the seeds in the middle of it. Then she began
to pull and push the dough around.

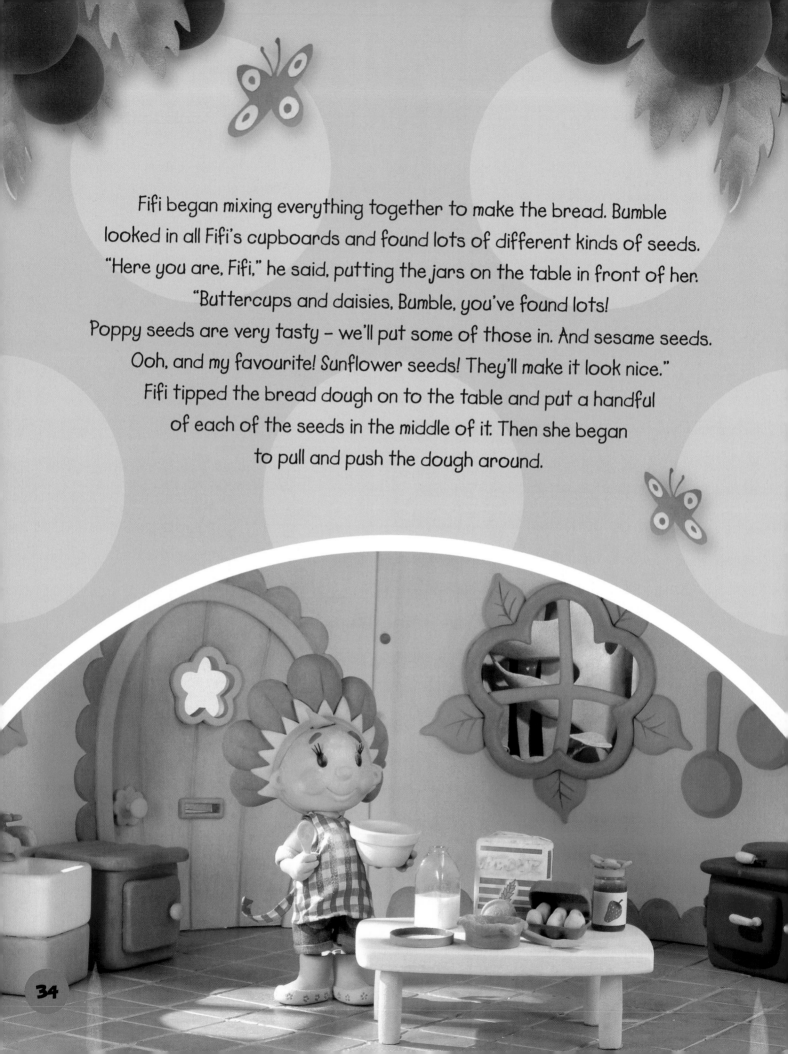

Bumble was puzzled. "What are you doing, Fifi?" he asked.

"I'm kneading the dough, Bumble," Fifi replied.

"You have to do this to help the bread rise properly."

"What shall we do while we're waiting, Fifi?" asked Bumble.

Fifi opened the kitchen window and put her hand out.

"Well, it seems to have stopped raining now," she said.

"The wind must have blown all the clouds away.

Shall we go for a walk and see if anyone else

would like to come over for tea?"

"Did someone say 'tea'?" buzzed a voice outside the window.

It was Stingo, hungry as usual! "Yes, Stingo, I did," laughed Fifi.

"And of course you're invited. But we have

to wait for the bread to rise,

so first you can help us

invite some more people!"

Primrose and Violet were very pleased to be invited.
They hadn't been shopping because of the rain and their food
cupboards were quite empty!
Stingo invited Slugsy, and then decided that was enough people
to share the delicious bread. "Don't want to risk not having enough
to go round!" he said. Poppy was just about to close
her Market Stall when Fifi and Bumble arrived.
"I'd love to come," she said,
"I've been very busy today, and I'm really hungry!"

Next was Aunt Tulip's House.
"Well, darlin'," said Aunt Tulip when
Fifi asked her. "Since you ask,
I'd love to! Thank you!"

Pip had been playing on his scooter when
the rain began, and was soaking wet.
"Thanks, Fifi," he said, "I'd love to come to tea.
Could I come early and dry off first, please?"
"Of course, you can, Pip," said Fifi,
"My oven's already heating up ready to bake
the bread, so the kitchen will be lovely
and warm by the time we get back.
Let's go and put the bread in now!"
"Golly Goosegogs! I'll help you!" said Pip,
excitedly. And off the three of them went,
back to Fifi's cottage.

"Now, where did I put the extra seeds?' said Fifi.
"Bumble, can you remember?"
"Fifi Forget-Me-Not Forgot!" laughed Bumble.
"You put them on the kitchen table, remember?"
"Did I?" giggled Fifi, and she went to get them.
But there was nothing there.
"I can't have put them there, Bumble.
They aren't there now."

"Well, I was sure you did, Fifi.
But maybe I was wrong.
Let's look for them."
So all three of them looked
around the kitchen, in the
cupboards, under the table –
even in the teapot, just in case!
But the seeds were
nowhere to be seen.
"Oh well, never mind," said Fifi,
the bread will be just
as tasty without them."

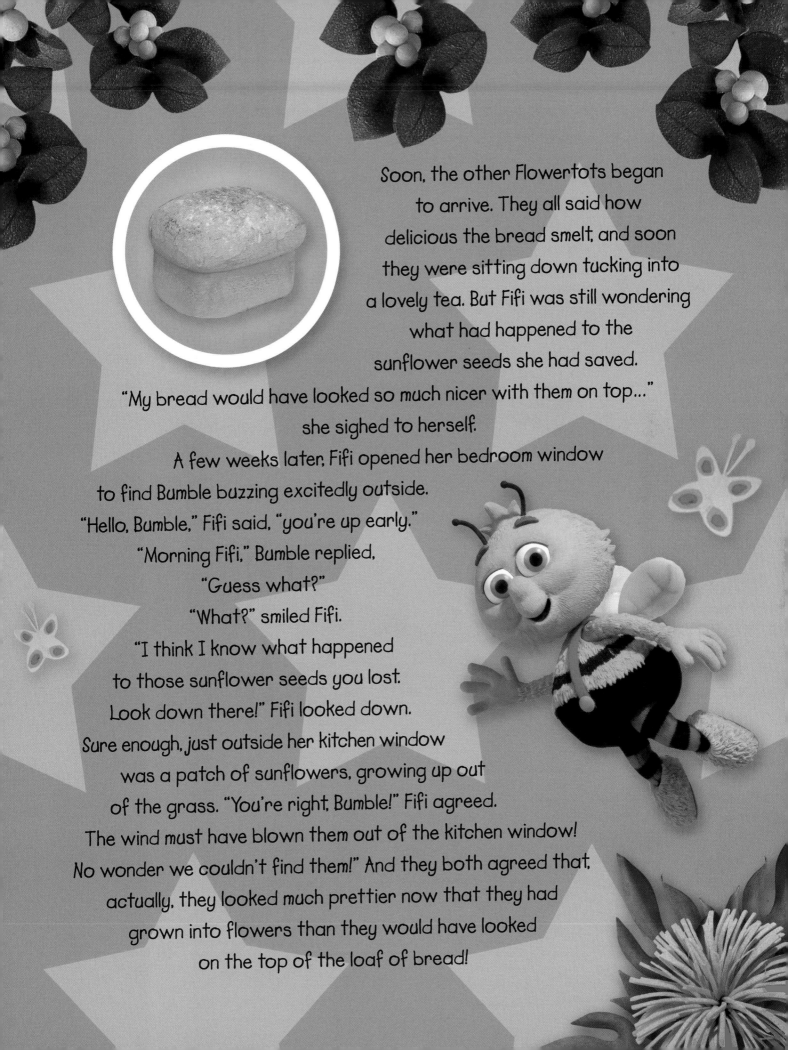

Soon, the other Flowertots began to arrive. They all said how delicious the bread smelt, and soon they were sitting down tucking into a lovely tea. But Fifi was still wondering what had happened to the sunflower seeds she had saved.

"My bread would have looked so much nicer with them on top..." she sighed to herself.

A few weeks later, Fifi opened her bedroom window to find Bumble buzzing excitedly outside.

"Hello, Bumble," Fifi said, "you're up early."

"Morning Fifi," Bumble replied, "Guess what?"

"What?" smiled Fifi.

"I think I know what happened to those sunflower seeds you lost. Look down there!" Fifi looked down. Sure enough, just outside her kitchen window was a patch of sunflowers, growing up out of the grass. "You're right, Bumble!" Fifi agreed. The wind must have blown them out of the kitchen window! No wonder we couldn't find them!" And they both agreed that, actually, they looked much prettier now that they had grown into flowers than they would have looked on the top of the loaf of bread!

New Clothes!

Here are some pictures of me in my everyday clothes, Diddly Dandelions, I would like some new outfits!

Would you design me some pretty new clothes? Fiddly Flowerpetals, the more colourful the better!

Puzzle Box

You can play this game with any number of friends. If there are just two of you, make a note of how quickly each of you guesses the object; the quickest is the winner each time. If there are more than two, take turns holding the box and have one guess each until someone gets in right. Then that person is the winner!

✿ Take an old shoe box with a lid and ask a friend to place a 'mystery object' inside and replace the lid, while you go outside the room (something that won't break!).

✿ Your friend should tape the lid closed, or tie a piece of string around it.

✿ Your must try to guess what's in it by sliding it from side to side, tapping it with a pencil, etc.

✿ The only thing you can't do is open it up and look inside!

✿ Take turns trying different objects and see who guesses the fastest!

Flowertot Maze

I've designed a special maze for you in Flowertot Garden.
See you if you can find your way through from
the arrow on the left, and meet me at the end!

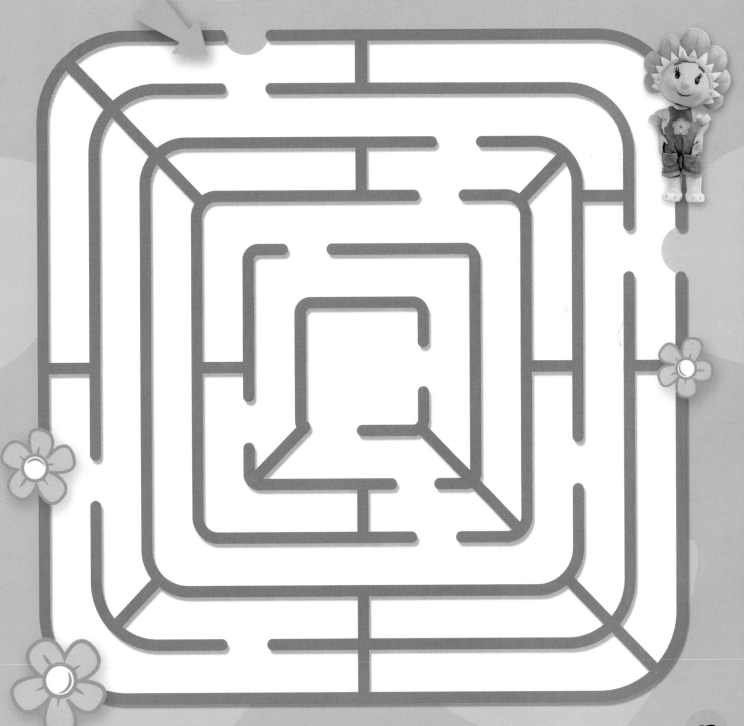

Think of a Colour!

Use these four boxes to list all the things you can think of that are the same colour; green, blue, yellow and pink.

Use pencil so that you can rub them out and play again, or draw your own borders on blank paper to make new lists with different colours!

Spot the Difference

Here are two pictures of me and my friend, Bumble. There are five differences between the two pictures. See if you can spot what they are and colour them in (the answers are upside-down at the bottom of the page!) Then colour in the rest of the pictures!

ANSWERS: Fifi's eyebrow is missing ✿ Bumble's button is coloured in ✿ Bumble's antennae is missing ✿ The flowers are missing from Fifi's welly boot ✿ A spot is missing from the strawberry

47

Make a Rainbow Bracelet

You will need:

Thin elastic in 6-inch (16 cm) lengths,
or long enough to fit loosely around
your wrist when tied together
Beads or buttons of different colours and sizes.

❀ Thread the beads or buttons on to the elastic, making
sure you don't put two of the same colour next to each other.

❀ Tie the ends of the elastic together so that the bracelet
will fit loosely around your wrist, but not fall off.

❀ You could make bracelets for all your friends, too!

❀ Or you could make a set of bracelets, using the same
colour beads or buttons for each bracelet,
and wear them all at once!

Make Your Own Beads

If you don't have enough beads or buttons, it's easy to make your own:

✿ Ask an adult for some hollow pasta, such as macaroni.

✿ Paint the outside of the pasta with your favourite colours.

✿ You can even make patterns with glue and sprinkle glitter
over them to make them even more lovely!

✿ When dry, use them just like ordinary beads, to make bracelets or necklaces.

✿ Another quick way of making beads is to roll coloured paper or card
into narrow tubes, gluing or taping the top edge all the way along.
Then you can cut them into short or long pieces.

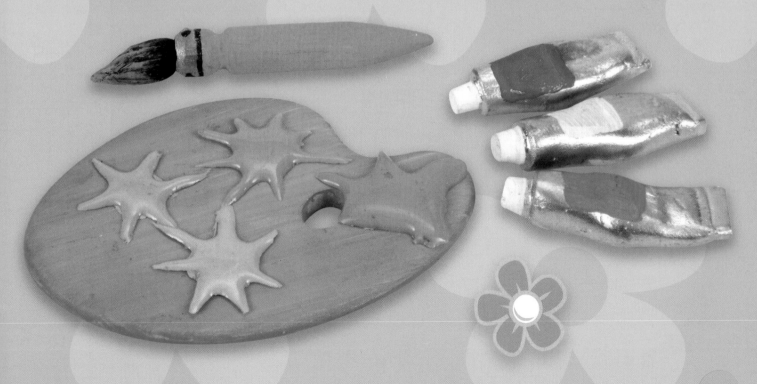

Colour In!

Here's a picture of me, Violet and Primrose – aren't we having fun!

Make a Rainbow Mobile

_ Paint or draw two rainbows, both the same, on the two pieces of card.

_ When they are dry, cut each stripe of colour out carefully.

_ Put one set of stripes in order, colour side down on a table, with a small gap between each one.

_ Put a dab of glue in the centre of each piece, and carefully lay the string on top, making sure it's right in the middle of each dab of glue. Leave enough string at the top to tie a loop in.

_ Now stick the other rainbow pieces on top, using more glue or tape if needed, facing the right way up.

_ Wait until the glue has dried, then tie a loop in the string. Hang your mobile up near a window and watch the colours spin in the breeze!

Goodbye!

Hope you enjoyed my annual –
don't forget to come back soon!